Now we know about...
BEING SAFE

Jinny Johnson

Crabtree Publishing Company
www.crabtreebooks.com

Published in Canada
Crabtree Publishing
616 Welland Avenue,
St. Catharines, Ontario
L2M 5V6

Published in the United States
Crabtree Publishing
PMB 16A,
350 Fifth Avenue, Suite 3308
New York, NY 10118

Editors: Belinda Weber, Lynn Peppas, Reagan Miller
Editorial director: Kathy Middleton
Production coordinator: Kenneth Wright
Prepress technician: Kenneth Wright
Studio manager: Sara Greasley
Designer: Trudi Webb
Production controller: Ed Green
Production manager: Suzy Kelly

Picture credits:
Getty Images: Altrendo Images: p. 18 (top right); Cornstock Images:
   p. 16 (left); Flying Colours: p. 18 (bottom left); JGI: p. 11 (top left)
Ghislain & Marie David de Lossy: p. 5 (bottom left)
iStock: front cover (top right), p. 5 (top), 6, 7 (bottom), 8, 10 (bottom),
   23 (bottom)
Shutterstock: front cover (bottom right and bottom left), back cover,
   p. 1, 4, 7 (top), 9, 10 (top), 11 (bottom right), 12, 13, 14–15, 16 (right),
   17, 19, 20 (bottom left), 21, 22, 23 (top)
Photolibrary.com: Somos Images: p. 20 (top right)
Hayley Terry: front cover (top left) and throughout

Every effort has been made to trace copyright holders, and we apologize in advance for any omissions. We would be pleased to insert the appropriate acknowledgments in any subsequent edition of this publication.

Library and Archives Canada Cataloguing in Publication

Johnson, Jinny
      Being safe / Jinny Johnson.

(Now we know about)
Includes index.
ISBN 978-0-7787-4717-8 (bound).--ISBN 978-0-7787-4734-5 (pbk.)

      1. Safety education--Juvenile literature.
2. Accidents--Prevention--Juvenile literature.
I. Title. II. Series: Now we know about (St. Catharines, Ont.)

HQ770.7.J64 2009   j613.6   C2009-903789-0

Library of Congress Cataloging-in-Publication Data

Johnson, Jinny.
   Being safe / Jinny Johnson.
      p. cm. -- (Now we know about)
   Includes index.
   ISBN 978-0-7787-4734-5 (pbk. : alk. paper) -- ISBN 978-0-7787-4717-8
(reinforced library binding : alk. paper)
   1. Safety education--Juvenile literature. 2. Accidents--Prevention--
Juvenile literature. I. Title. II. Series.

HQ770.7.J64 2010
613.6083--dc22

                                                                 2009024183

Published in 2010 by Crabtree Publishing Company

All rights reserved. No part of this publication may be reproduced, copied, stored in a retrieval system or transmitted in any form or by any means electronic, mechanical, photocopying, recording or otherwise without prior written permission of the copyright owner. Copyright © ticktock Entertainment Ltd 2009

Contents

How do I stay safe at home? 4

Staying safe in the kitchen 6

How do I stay safe in the bathroom? 8

Fire! 10

Online safety 12

How do I cross the road safely? 14

Staying safe in cars and on bikes 16

Stranger danger 18

Staying safe outdoors 20

Being around animals 22

Glossary/Index 24

How do I stay safe at home?

We feel safe at home. But you would be surprised how many accidents happen at home.

Danger!

Guns and knives are **dangerous**. They could hurt you very badly. Do not touch a gun or knife. If you find a gun or knife, tell an adult right away.

Bottles and pills

Never take any pills you find, even if they look like candy. Never drink anything from a bottle. Check with an adult first. It might not be what it says on the label.

Medicines should be locked in a cupboard.

pills

Watch out for windows

Never lean out of an open window. It is very easy to fall. Never climb or play on **windowsills**.

Be careful when looking out of windows.

Playing on stairs

Do not play on the stairs. Be careful when going up or down them so you do not fall. Do not leave your toys on the stairs. Someone else might trip and fall over them.

Do not play with your toys on the staircase.

Talking Point

Why is it dangerous to climb on furniture?

Furniture looks strong. But it could fall over or break if you climb on it. You could fall and hurt yourself. Climb in the playground only. The climbers there are built for you to climb on!

WORD WIZARD!
adult
Grown-up person

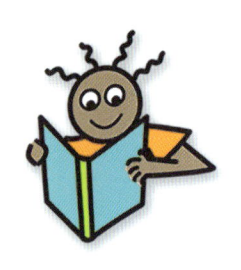

Staying safe in the kitchen

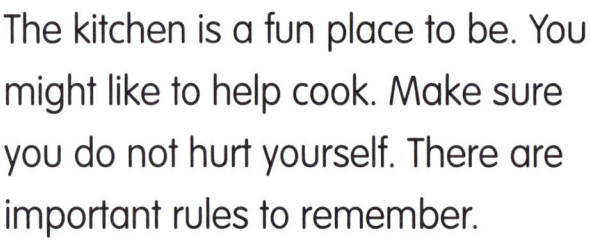

The kitchen is a fun place to be. You might like to help cook. Make sure you do not hurt yourself. There are important rules to remember.

Kitchen know-how

Always be careful around the oven. Make sure an adult is with you if you want to cook something. Ask an adult to turn the oven on for you.

Always ask an adult to help you carry hot dishes or take things out of the oven.

Pots and pans

Never touch pots and pans. They might be very hot. Adults use oven mitts when removing pots from the stove.

Talking point

Why is it important to wash your hands before cooking or eating?

Always wash your hands before you touch food or eat anything. You want to make sure your hands do not have **germs** or dirt on them. If you touch food that is raw make sure to wash your hands again before eating anything.

Ask how

Always ask before you use electrical equipment. Get an adult to help show you how. If you use the microwave make sure you know what dishes are safe to put in it.

Keep safe in the kitchen. Always ask an adult to help you cook.

WORD WIZARD!
raw
Food that is fresh and has not been cooked

7

How do I stay safe in the bathroom?

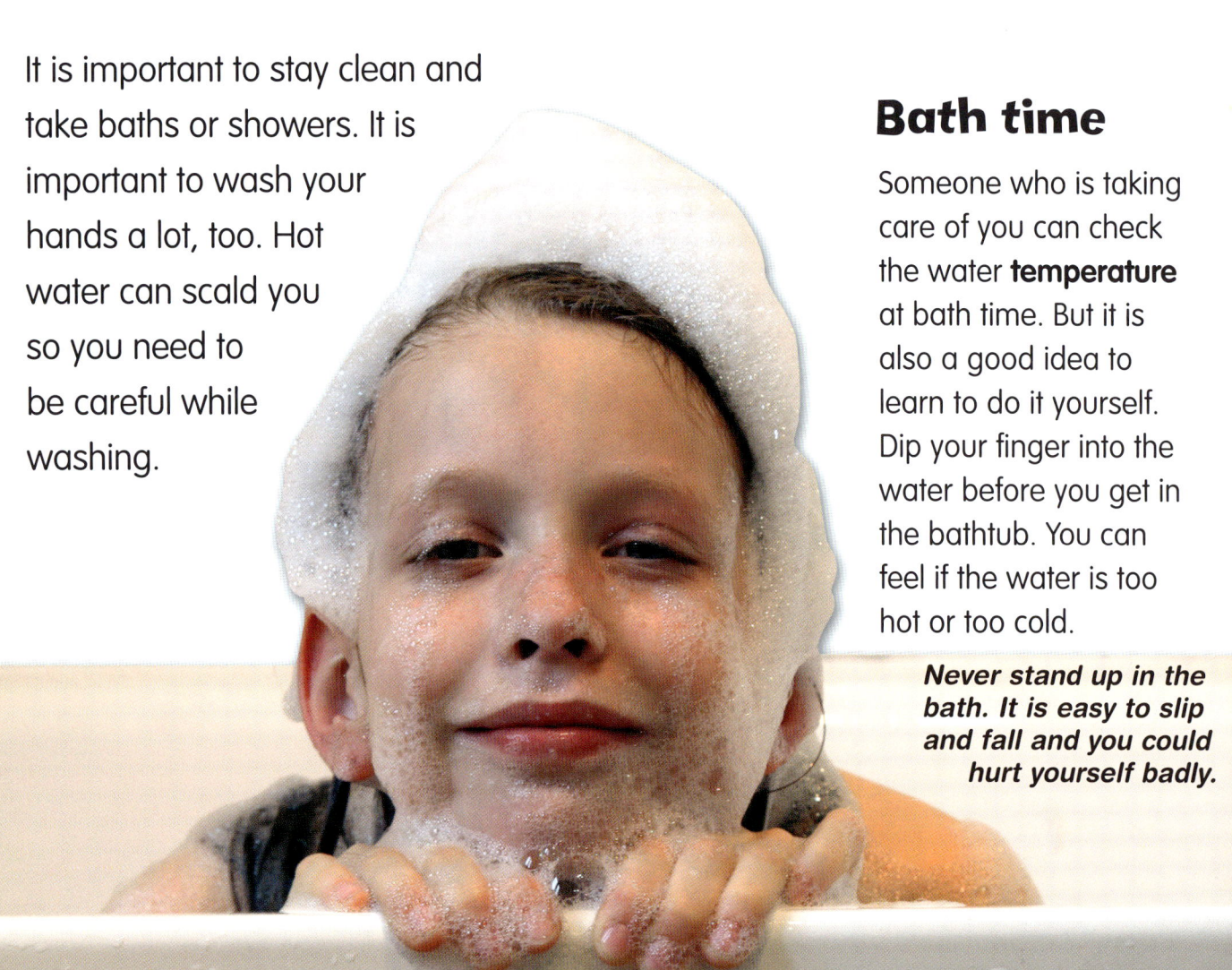

It is important to stay clean and take baths or showers. It is important to wash your hands a lot, too. Hot water can scald you so you need to be careful while washing.

Bath time

Someone who is taking care of you can check the water **temperature** at bath time. But it is also a good idea to learn to do it yourself. Dip your finger into the water before you get in the bathtub. You can feel if the water is too hot or too cold.

Never stand up in the bath. It is easy to slip and fall and you could hurt yourself badly.

Think about others

Other people use the bathroom after you. Put the toilet seat down before you flush the toilet. Keep it down. This helps stop germs from spreading.

Clean hands

Turn the cold water tap on first when you wash your hands. That way you will not get burned by hot water.

Use the cold water first.

Talking Point

What are the biggest dangers in the bathroom?

Water splashes can make the bathroom floor slippery. Take special care that you do not slip and fall. Use a towel to wipe up any water you spill on the floor.

WORD WIZARD!
scald
Burn caused by hot water

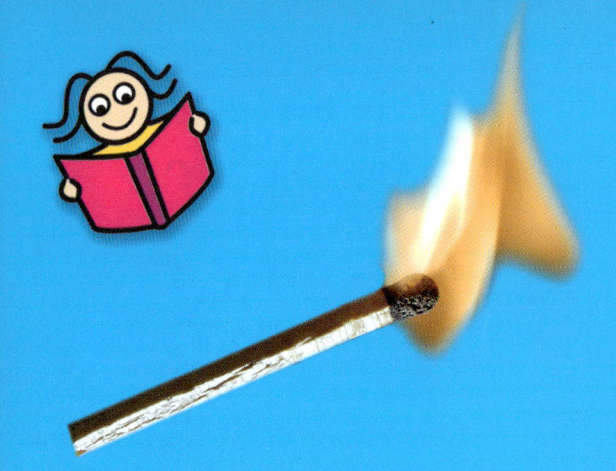

Fire!

A fire is one of the most dangerous things that can happen in any home. But you can do a lot to stop them.

Here is what not to do

Do not play with matches. Never touch lighters or candles.

Do not put clothes or other things over a lamp or heater.

Do not stand close to an open fire or oven. Your clothes might catch on fire.

Do not stick things into electrical sockets or play with wires.

Fires should always have a guard.

smoke alarm

What is a smoke alarm?

A **smoke alarm** can sense if there is smoke in the air. It makes a loud, beeping noise. This sound warns you to get out of the house. Ask your parents if you have smoke alarms in your home.

Talking Point

Why do you need a smoke alarm?

It is important to have smoke alarms in your home. You might not know there is a fire, especially if it is at night. A smoke alarm tells you right away if there is a fire. It warns you so you can get out safely.

What if there is a fire?

If a fire starts, leave your home as quickly and carefully as possible. Do not stop to get your toys or go back for anything. Make a fire escape plan with your family. This plan will help everyone know what to do in case there is a fire.

Make a fire escape plan.

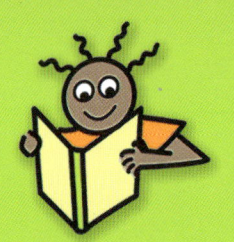

Online safety

Working on a computer is fun. You can learn a lot, too. But you have to take care. Ask your parents or caregivers to help you use **email** and the Internet safely. They can help you choose safe **search engines** and **chat rooms** to visit.

Do not give anyone your name. Never plan to meet someone without asking your parents, or caregivers, first.

Can I give my name and address online?

Never give out any information about you or your family online. Do not tell anyone online your name, where you live, or your phone number. If someone asks you these questions, tell a caregiver right away.

What if someone asks to meet me?

Tell your parents right away. If they say it is all right, you could meet the person. Make sure your parents or caregivers come with you if you do. Make sure it is at a place where there are a lot of people around.

Tell your parents if someone online makes you feel scared.

Talking Point

Can you chat with friends on the Internet?

You can chat with your friends on the Internet, but check with your parents first. Let them know who you are chatting with. Only chat with people online that you know in real life. That way you will stay safe.

What if I get a nasty email?

Do not reply or send an email back to them. Tell your parents. If it happens again they can get in touch with your email service. If you see a site that you think is wrong, tell your parents. It can happen to anyone. It is not your fault.

How do I cross the road safely?

You probably always go out with an adult, but it is important to know how to cross the road safely.

Crossing the road

Find a safe place to cross. A special crossing with **traffic signals** is best. If there is no special crossing find a place where you can see all around you. Never cross near a car, bus, or large truck.

Look both ways!

Listen!

Stop, look, listen

Stop at the curb. Do not stand too close to the edge. Look both ways to see if anything is coming. Listen carefully, too. Sometimes you can hear traffic coming before you see it. Look again. Walk across the road when you know it is safe. Look and listen while you walk.

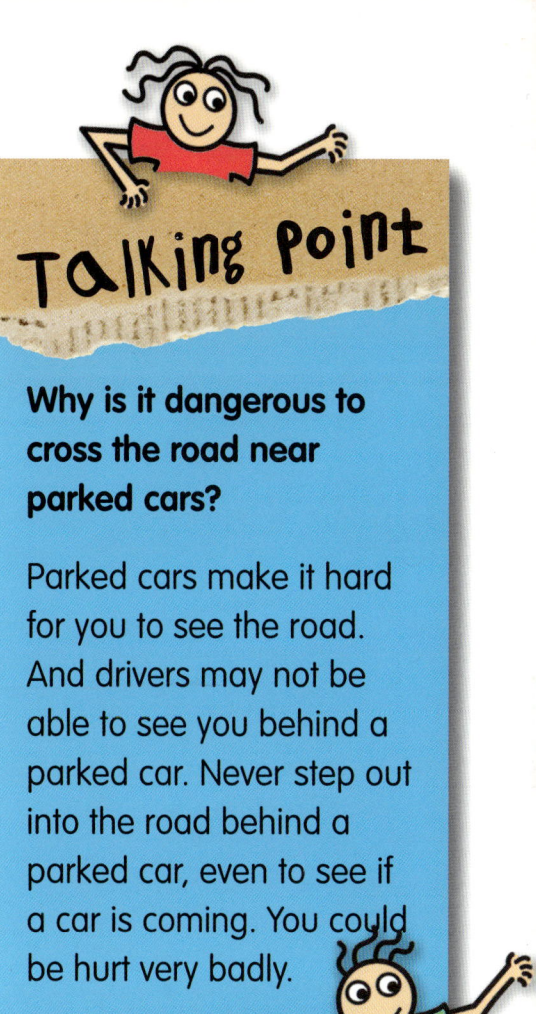

Talking Point

Why is it dangerous to cross the road near parked cars?

Parked cars make it hard for you to see the road. And drivers may not be able to see you behind a parked car. Never step out into the road behind a parked car, even to see if a car is coming. You could be hurt very badly.

Do not run

Do not run across the road. You could fall and not get up in time if a car is coming.

Staying safe in cars and on bikes

Always sit in the back seat of a car. It is much safer than the front. Make sure you are strapped in. This means you will not be thrown if the car stops suddenly.

seat belt

Sit up

You will need to sit on a special car seat until you are bigger. Always wear your **seat belt**. Help your parents or caregivers by making sure any other children in the car wear their seat belts too.

Always wear a helmet and bright clothing when riding your bike.

16

How do I stay safe on a bike?

Always wear a **helmet** when you ride a bike. It protects your head if you fall or have an accident. Wear bright colors so others can see you easily.

How can I help my parents keep us safe in the car?

A driver has to watch the road all the time. You can help by being quiet in the car. Never throw things around. Never shout or scream.

Talking Point

Why do you have to wear a seat belt in the car?

A seat belt is made to hold you safely in your seat. The belt tightens around you if the car stops suddenly. This stops you from getting thrown forward into the front seats or window.

Stay inside

Never open the door when the car is moving or lean out a window. Do not even put your hand out of the window. You never know what might come past.

Stranger danger

Do not talk to people you do not know. Stay well away from strangers who try to talk to you or give you candy. If someone does try, tell an adult you know right away.

Never take candy from strangers.

Do not talk to strangers

Your parents will let you and your teachers know if someone you know is coming to pick you up from school. If a stranger tells you your mother or father asked him or her to pick you up, walk away fast. Tell a teacher right away. Yell as loud as you can if someone tries to grab you.

Never go near a stranger's car.

Do not help

If a stranger asks you for help say no. It might seem like a mean thing to do but do not worry. It is the right thing to do. If a stranger needs help doing something then he or she can ask another adult.

Talking Point

Why should you not talk to strangers?

Most people are nice. But some people might want to hurt you. If you do not know someone it is hard to know if they are being friendly. Only stop and talk to people you know. That way you will be safe and not have any trouble from strangers.

WORD WIZARD!
stranger
A person that you do not know

Staying safe outdoors

It is great to play outside. You might be lucky enough to have a garden of your own or a park close by where you can go.

playing in a pool

Water safety

Do not play near water unless an adult is with you. Never go swimming by yourself.

Safe sun

Wear **sunscreen** if you play outside in hot weather. Ask a parent or caregiver for help putting it on so you do not get a **sunburn**. Wear a hat and some **sunglasses**, too.

Poisonous plants

Never eat a plant you find outside. A lot of plants have leaves, **berries**, or flowers that are poisonous. That means they can make you sick. Always wash your hands after touching plants.

You can look at berries, but do not touch!

Playgrounds are safe places to have fun.

Talking Point

Can you get a sunburn on a cloudy day?

Yes, you can get a sunburn on a cloudy day. It is important to protect your skin from the Sun in the hot, summer months. Make sure to put on sunscreen if you are playing outdoors. Wear a long-sleeved shirt and hat.

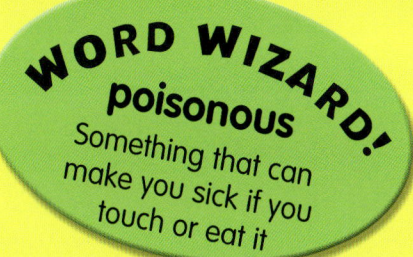

WORD WIZARD!
poisonous
Something that can make you sick if you touch or eat it

21

Being around animals

Cats, dogs, and other pets are a lot of fun. But they need to be treated in the right way. Even the nicest pets can get angry sometimes. They might even scratch or bite.

Be polite

You would never rush up to a kid you did not know and start petting them. So do not do this to a dog. Many dogs are friendly but some might get scared of strangers. They may bite. Always ask the dog's owner before petting the dog.

WORD WIZARD!
sting
Painful wound made by an insect

Let the dog smell you before you pet it.

Never try to touch an animal that is caring for its young or eating. Never tease or shout at an animal.

Wild creatures

Do not go near wild animals such as snakes. Never try to poke an insect nest. The insects could sting you.

wasps' nest

Do not kiss animals or let them touch your face.

Talking Point

When is it safe to pet an animal?

You should never pet an animal without first asking its owner. You should ask the owner even if you know him or her and have seen the animal before. Never grab an animal or shout. You might frighten it.

Always wash your hands after touching animals.

Glossary

berries Small, juicy fruits. Some berries are poisonous so do not touch or eat any without first checking with an adult

chat room An Internet site where users can talk to each other using instant messages

dangerous Something that could cause you harm

email A message sent from one computer to another

germ Something that can make you sick

helmet A hard hat that protects your head

search engine A special program that helps you find things on the Internet

seat belt A belt that is attached to a car seat

sunburn A rash on the skin caused by too much Sun

sunscreen Cream that helps protect your skin from a sunburn

sunglasses Glasses with special tinted lens that help protect your eyes from the Sun

smoke alarm A machine that detects smoke in the air and makes a loud noise

temperature A measure of how hot or cold something is

traffic signals Lights that tell the road users when it is safe to drive or walk on the road

windowsill The ledge at the base of a window frame

Index

A
animals 22–23
B
baths 8, 9
C
chat rooms 12
computers 12–13
cookers 6, 10
E
emails 12, 13
F
fires 10–11

G
germs 7, 9
guns 4
H
helmets 16, 17
I
insects 22, 23
Internet 12, 13
K
knives 4, 7
M
medicines 4
microwaves 7

O
oven mitts 7
P
pans 7
pills 4
plants 21
pots 7
S
search engines 12
seat belts 16, 17
showers 8
smoke alarms 11

sockets 10
strangers 18–19, 22
sunburn 20, 21
sunscreen 20, 21
sunglasses 20
swimming 20
T
toys 5, 11
traffic signals 14
W
water 8, 9, 20
windows 5, 17

Printed in the U.S.A.—CG